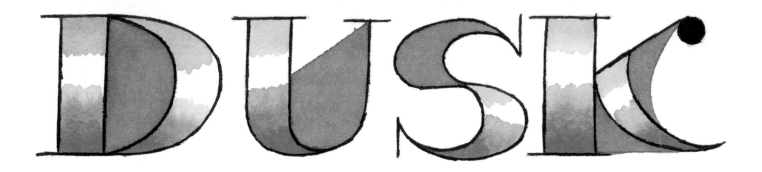

Uri Shulevitz

Margaret Ferguson Books

FARRAR STRAUS GIROUX

New York

Farrar Straus Giroux Books for Young Readers
175 Fifth Avenue, New York 10010

Color separations by Bright Arts (H.K.) Ltd.
Printed in the United States of America by Phoenix Color Corp.
d/b/a Lehigh Phoenix, Hagerstown, Maryland
Designed by Roberta Pressel
First edition, 2013
10 9 8 7 6 5 4 3 2 1

mackids.com

Library of Congress Cataloging-in-Publication Data
Shulevitz, Uri, 1935— author, illustrator.
    Dusk / Uri Shulevitz. — First edition.
      pages cm.
    Summary: "Boy with dog and grandfather with beard watch holiday
lights turn on in the city"—Provided by publisher.
    ISBN 978-0-374-31903-8 (hardcover)
    [1. City and town life—Fiction.   2. Night—Fiction.]   I. Title.

PZ7.S5594Du 2013
[E]—dc23
                            2012045967

Farrar Straus Giroux Books for Young Readers may be purchased for
business or promotional use. For information on bulk purchases please
contact Macmillan Corporate and Premium Sales Department at
(800) 221-7945 x5442 or by email at specialmarkets@macmillan.com.

For Paula

Winter.
Days are short.
Nights are long.

Boy with dog and grandfather with beard go for a walk.

When they come to the river,

the sun is starting to sink.

"It's getting dark," said boy with dog. "How sad, the day is no more."
"Dusk," said grandfather with beard.

When they go back to the city,

people are hurrying. Some home.

Others, to shop.

"I swear I declare
I'll search here and there.
I'll search till I find
the best of its kind.
Toys for my girls
and toys for my boys,"
said man with cravat.

"Today's no time for
chitchat!
Tomatoes, potatoes,
and food for my cat,
my kitty, my sweetie,
my kitty cat,"
said woman with hat.

"I'll skip, I'll jump, I'll run.
I won't pause, I won't rest
till I find the sweetest,
   the best.
Candies for Mandy
and cookies for Randy,"
said retired acrobat.

"Dusky musky, dusky zdat,
kholidaysky ikla zat,
sveet candoosky ikla
    bloosky,
bedy funnye ikla zdat,"
said visitor from planet
    Zataplat.

Buildings grow darker.

Skies grow dimmer.

As nature's lights go out,

city's lights come on.
First one,

then others,

then more,

and more.

Lights

there

and there.

Lights,

lights,

everywhere.

"It's as light as day," said the boy.